Library of Congress Cataloging in Publication Data: Cosgrove, Stephen. Giggle. (A Whimsie storybook) SUMMARY: One look in Switch Witch's magic mirror convinces Strawberry that she is the most beautiful creature in the land. 1. Children's stories, American. [1. Pride and vanity—Fiction. 2. Witches—Fiction.] I. Reasoner, Charles, ill. II. Title. III. Series: Cosgrove, Stephen. Whimsie storybook. PZ7.C8187Gg 1985 [E] 85-42716 ISBN: 0-394-87458-7

Manufactured in Belgium
1 2 3 4 5 6 7 8 9 0

The Whimsies STORYBOOKS ™

Giggle

by Stephen Cosgrove

illustrated by Charles Reasoner

Random House New York

Have you ever watched a butterfly as it flitted on a summer wind? If you could follow that butterfly until it finally came to light, you would find yourself in the magical, mystical Land of Whim.

In this land of gentle breezes lived laughing little creatures called Whimsies. They worked here and they played here. They slept here and they dreamed here. For this was and always would be the home of the Whimsies beside the River Whim, beneath the Quirk Mountains.

The Whimsies had cute button noses and bright, shiny eyes, and were covered from head to foot with fur as soft as dandelion down. They were very beautiful in their own special Whimsie way. But to say they were beautiful is not to say they were perfect, for they were not.

There was old Cap'n Grump, who clumped about town on a wooden leg. He wasn't perfect, but he was beautiful in his own special way.

There were Blossom and Sprout, the Whimsie twins who were just a bit overweight. They were not perfect, but they were beautiful in their own way.

There was Woolly Woofer, the Whimsies' only dog, who was frequently dusty or muddy from rolling on the ground, but he, too, was beautiful in his own special way.

Of all the Whimsies there was only one who did appear perfect in every way. Her name was Strawberry and she was as kind as she was beautiful. She loved to wander through town saying nice things to all her Whimsie friends. She would help old Cap'n Grump sit down on his favorite

log in the park. She would compliment Blossom about her choice of ribbons for the day. And she always stopped to give Woolly Woofer a soft and gentle pat on his furry head.

Strawberry was the delight of everyone in the Land of Whim.

Every day at five to four, Strawberry would take a long walk through Fiddle Forest. She would smell the beautiful flowers and watch the little wingless birds called Hoppers who chirped about her legs.

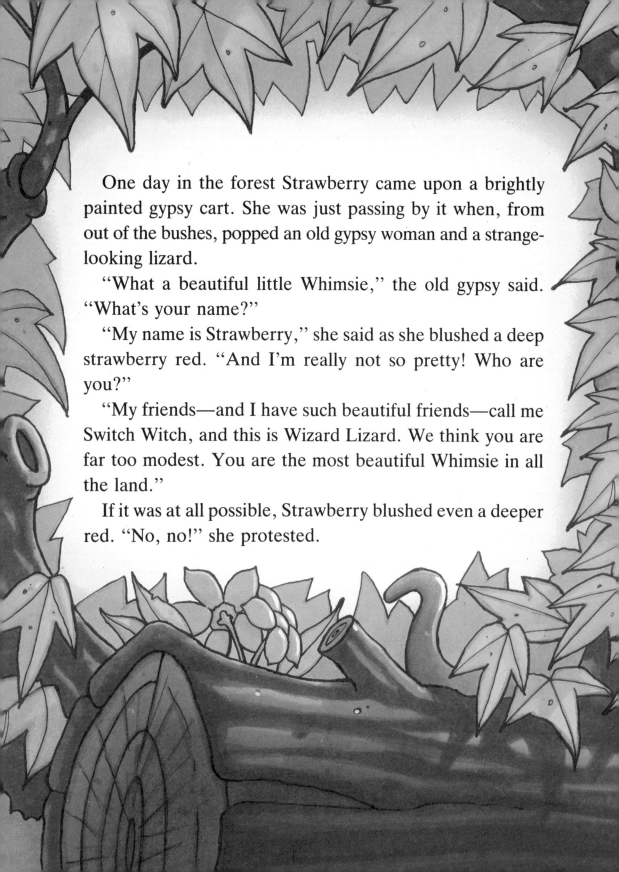

One day in the forest Strawberry came upon a brightly painted gypsy cart. She was just passing by it when, from out of the bushes, popped an old gypsy woman and a strange-looking lizard.

"What a beautiful little Whimsie," the old gypsy said. "What's your name?"

"My name is Strawberry," she said as she blushed a deep strawberry red. "And I'm really not so pretty! Who are you?"

"My friends—and I have such beautiful friends—call me Switch Witch, and this is Wizard Lizard. We think you are far too modest. You are the most beautiful Whimsie in all the land."

If it was at all possible, Strawberry blushed even a deeper red. "No, no!" she protested.

"You know your problem, little Whimsie? You have never taken a good look at your own beauty." The old witch reached into the cart and held up a round golden mirror. "Here, little Whimsie, look into the Magic Mirror and you'll never be the same."

Strawberry took the beautiful mirror carefully in her hands and quickly looked at her reflection. She looked once, she looked twice, and then she looked again. The mirror *was* magic. Her fur had never looked so pink and fluffy. Her eyes had never looked so shiny. "Why, I *am* pretty! In fact, I'm beautiful. Why, next to me, everybody else is really ugly!"

Switch Witch giggled wickedly as Strawberry walked away, never once taking her eyes off her reflection in the Magic Mirror.

As Strawberry went back through Fiddle Forest, she came upon the Hoppers. They flittered and hopped about her legs as usual, playing their silly games.

Strawberry took one look at them and began to giggle.

"Ugly birds without any wings, you're so ugly you can't even sing!" She broke into gales of giggles as she continued on her way, leaving some very hurt little birds hopping sadly about in Fiddle Forest.

Strawberry had just reached town and was looking at herself in her special mirror again when up clumped old Cap'n Grump. She took one look at him and then burst into giggles. "Peg leg! Peg leg! Cap'n Grump's got a wooden leg!" she chanted.

Poor Cap'n Grump just leaned on his cane and looked awfully surprised and sad as Strawberry skipped on her way.

Strawberry skipped up the street, all the while looking at herself in the Magic Mirror. She was so enchanted by her own reflection that she didn't see Blossom and Sprout, who were walking home from school. With a great big bump they all collided and fell into a heap.

Strawberry looked at Blossom, then at Sprout, and began to giggle. Blossom and Sprout joined in the laughter. All three Whimsies laughed and laughed until they could laugh no more. Finally Blossom asked, "But . . . what are we laughing at?"

Strawberry giggled. "Blossom and Sprout . . . short and stout. They're so fat you'd better look out!" With that she dusted herself off, looked at herself in the mirror, and went giggling on her way.

The Whimsie twins sat in the road as large tears slid down their furry cheeks.

"Why is Strawberry acting so mean?" they wondered.

Strawberry was so caught up in her own beauty that she couldn't see the hurt she was spreading all over the Land of Whim. With a giddy giggle, she shouted to Woolly Woofer, "Clip-clop, flip-flop, Woolly looks like an old dust mop!"

And again she peeked at her own reflection and skipped off on her way.

Woolly was so hurt that he dropped his favorite bone and fell into a sad, fluffy heap.

Nearly every Whimsie had been hurt by the giggling insults of Strawberry. Finally, old Cap'n Grump stopped her on rickety Branch Bridge. "Why, hello, Strawberry," he said. "You look very pretty today!"

Strawberry looked at him once, then again, and began

to giggle. "Why, of course I do. I am the most beautiful Whimsie in all the Land of Whim!"

"Oh, I see," said old Cap'n Grump. "Where did you get that mirror?"

"It was given to me by an old gypsy," Strawberry told him.

"Ahh, Switch Witch," said the old Whimsie, "and her Magic Mirror! Did you know there is more magic beyond the mirror? To see your real reflection you only have to look into the eyes of those Whimsies around you."

Strawberry looked at her reflection mirrored in the eyes of the old captain. She was shocked. What she saw was not the most beautiful Whimsie in all the Land of Whim but a selfish, giggling monster.

Strawberry felt very, very sorry for what she had done. With a lump in her throat she threw the Magic Mirror into the River Whim.

As for the Magic Mirror, it would have remained lost forever had not Wizard Lizard gone to the River Whim for a sip of cool, clean water. He peered down, and all at once he saw his reflection in the Magic Mirror lying on the sandy bottom. "Why," he croaked and giggled, picking up the mirror, "I am the most beautiful creature in all the Land of Whim!"

He gaily skipped and giggled back to Switch Witch Castle and the Land of Frippery, chanting "Switch Witch! Switch Witch! She's so ugly, she makes me itch!"

All returned to normal in the Land of Whim. Once again Strawberry was her sweet, gentle self, and life went on as it always had.

Strawberry laughs
And Strawberry
giggles,
But never at a worm
For the way that it
wiggles.